A Second Birth

Ariel Mitchell

A SAMUEL FRENCH ACTING EDITION

SAMUEL FRENCH

FOUNDED 1830

SAMUELFRENCH.COM
SAMUELFRENCH-LONDON.CO.UK

ISBN 978-0-573-70216-7

www.SamuelFrench.com
www.SamuelFrench-London.co.uk

FOR PRODUCTION ENQUIRIES

UNITED STATES AND CANADA
Info@SamuelFrench.com
1-866-598-8449

UNITED KINGDOM AND EUROPE
Plays@SamuelFrench-London.co.uk
020-7255-4302

Each title is subject to availability from Samuel French, depending upon country of performance. Please be aware that *A SECOND BIRTH* may not be licensed by Samuel French in your territory. Professional and amateur producers should contact the nearest Samuel French office or licensing partner to verify availability.

MUSIC USE NOTE

Licensees are solely responsible for obtaining formal written permission from copyright owners to use copyrighted music in the performance of this play and are strongly cautioned to do so. If no such permission is obtained by the licensee, then the licensee must use only original music that the licensee owns and controls. Licensees are solely responsible and liable for all music clearances and shall indemnify the copyright owners of the play(s) and their licensing agent, Samuel French, against any costs, expenses, losses and liabilities arising from the use of music by licensees. Please contact the appropriate music licensing authority in your territory for the rights to any incidental music.

IMPORTANT BILLING AND CREDIT REQUIREMENTS

If you have obtained performance rights to this title, please refer to your licensing agreement for important billing and credit requirements.

A SECOND BIRTH was first produced by Brigham Young University in the Margetts Theatre on September 25, 2012. The performance was directed by George Nelson, with sets by Rory Scanlon and Brent Robinson, costumes by Joceyln Chatman, lights by Graham Whipple, sound and music composition by Troy Sales, and make-up design by Jennifer Beal and Celena Kurogi. The production stage manager was Brett Vandygriff. The cast was as follows:

NASIM/NASIMA . . . . Marcella Toronto
YASIR. . . . . David Lee
LAILA . . . . .Jennifer Chandler
AZADEH . . . . Noelle Houston
HODA . . . . .Briana Shipley
ZEMAN . . . . Devin Wadsworth
MR. RAFAAT . . . . Moises B. Lopez

A SECOND BIRTH received its first stage reading on February 11, 2011 at the LA Theatre Center, in Los Angeles, California. The play was a National Semi-Finalist in the 2011 Kennedy Center American College Theater Festival.

A SECOND BIRTH was also awarded the Vera Hinckley Mayhew Award for Playwriting at Brigham Young University in April 2011.

A shortened version of the play, directed by Kristie Post Wallace, was produced and performed as a forty minute Mask Club at Brigham Young University in October 2011.

A SECOND BIRTH premiered at Brigham Young University on September 25, 2012.

In 2013, the play was awarded the Harold and Mimi Steinberg National Student Playwriting Award and third place for the David Mark Cohen Award.

CHARACTERS

NASIM/NASIMA – (Nah-seem/Nah-seem-meh), 17, a bright young girl who has been raised as a boy since the age of 5

YASIR – (Yah-s-air), 18, an athletic, fun loving teenage boy, Nasim's best friend

LAILA – (Lie-la), 16, Yasir's sister and Nasima's friend since childhood

AZADEH – (Az-ah-day), 15, Nasima's sister

HODA – (Hoe-dah), Nasima's Mother

ZEMAN – (Zeh-mon), Nasima's Father

MR. RAFAAT – (Mr. Rah-fah-aht), a shopkeeper and family friend

SETTING

YASIR's House
NASIMA's House
MR. RAFAAT's Store
The Bridge

TIME

Somewhere in Afghanistan. Modern day.

AUTHOR'S NOTES

All characters appearing in this play are purely fictitious. Any resemblance to real persons, living or dead, is coincidental.

The events and scenes of the play are inventions of the playwright created and adapted with critical input from friends, readers, mentors and suggestions made in public readings, discussions, and workshops. The contemporary practice of *bacha posh* is accepted in some areas of the Islamic Middle East.

ACKNOWLEDGEMENTS

I would like to thank my parents for their support, encouragement, and inspiration; KCACTF Region VIII for recognition and professional criticism; Roger Sorensen and his cast for the work they put into the KCACTF reading; Eric Samuelson for many helpful comments and criticisms; Mary Farhanakian for cultural notes; Kristie Post Wallace, her cast, and crew for the marvelous first student production and feedback; BYU's Fall 2011 WDA class for pulling this play out of me and for all of the very helpful improv; Kate Forsythe, the most amazing dramaturg a playwright could ask for; and George Nelson (who I can never possibly repay or thank) for tireless reading, critiquing, suggesting, and for never letting me off easy – always believing I could do better when I thought I was finished.

Thank you.

ACT I

(The lights come up on YASIR*'s house: a modern, well-furnished living room of a home in Afghanistan. Two boys,* YASIR*, 18, and* NASIM*, 17, are leaning over a table with paper and books spread out in front of them.)*

NASIM. Good. Next?

*(*NASIM *picks up a soccer ball and starts playing with it.)*

YASIR. Need to find the length of AB. It's a right triangle. Sine of theta is six-tenths.

NASIM. All right. Now you...

YASIR. Set it up. Sine is...um...

NASIM. Op –

YASIR. Opposite over hypotenuse.

NASIM. Good.

YASIR. So...(*works it out on his paper*) Like that?

NASIM. Forgot to take the square root.

*(*YASIR *groans.)*

It's simple.

YASIR. For you.

NASIM. Just set up the formula and go through the steps. Try the next one.

*(*YASIR *grabs for the ball.)*

YASIR. Let's take a break.

*(*NASIM *pulls the ball out of* YASIR*'s reach.)*

NASIM. After this problem.

YASIR. When am I ever going to use trigonometry anyway?

NASIM. You're going to university.

YASIR. You should apply. Let my father talk to yours.

NASIM. Like that'll help.

YASIR. He's very persuasive.

NASIM. He'd only make it worse.

YASIR. Why?

NASIM. Does your father like anyone meddling in his affairs?

YASIR. An education would help. You wouldn't have to be stuck in that dumb store for the rest of your life.

(pause)

Have you gained weight?

*(**NASIM** looks down at his chest and quickly turns away.)*

NASIM. No!

YASIR. You sure? You're looking a little…

*(**NASIM** points at the textbook.)*

NASIM. Quit stalling.

*(**YASIR** reluctantly sits down and works out the next problem.)*

*(**NASIM** crosses away from **YASIR**, tugging at his shirt.)*

YASIR. How's that?

*(**NASIM** returns to the table and looks over **YASIR**'s work.)*

NASIM. Good…until here.

*(**YASIR**'s younger sister **LAILA**, 16, enters in a floor-length skirt and headscarf, carrying a tray of snacks and tea. **YASIR** glances at her, then back at **NASIM**.)*

YASIR. Better than last time.

NASIM. That's not saying much.

*(**YASIR** closes his book and pushes it away.)*

At this rate, we'll miss prayer.

*(**LAILA** sets down the tea.)*

YASIR. You worry too much.

NASIM. You don't worry enough!

YASIR. At least I can hang onto a ball...

NASIM. I was side tackled!

(YASIR takes a cup from LAILA.)

YASIR. If it makes you feel better.

(NASIM takes a cup from LAILA.)

NASIM. Football doesn't really matter.

YASIR. Because you're not good at it...

NASIM. Hey!

YASIR. Without me you'd never have any fun.

NASIM. Not true!

(pause)

All right. Maybe a little...

(Handing LAILA back his cup)

Thanks.

YASIR. (*Mimicking* NASIM) Thanks.

NASIM. Can we get back to work?

(LAILA picks up the tray, sticks her tongue out at YASIR, and exits.)

YASIR. We'll miss prayer!

NASIM. You're going to have to finish these sometime.

(YASIR grabs the ball.)

YASIR. Not if I can help it.

(runs out)

You coming?

(YASIR exits. NASIM follows behind.)

Scene Two

(NASIM's house. The furnishings are more modest than those in the previous scene. ZEMAN, NASIM's father, finishes praying in a corner of the room.)

ZEMAN. Allah, praised be thy name. I'm so grateful. I've been blessed with thy word and the opportunity to raise my family by thy teachings…

(NASIM's mother, HODA enters, trying not to disturb ZEMAN.)

Allah, I seek thy guidance and aid in what thou wills. I ask for courage which only thou can bestow…Allah, the most kind, the most merciful. Ameen. (*Pronouced: Ah-mean*)

(ZEMAN looks up, noticing HODA.)

Is Nasim back?

HODA. Still tutoring.

ZEMAN. It's getting late.

(ZEMAN takes out some work.)

HODA. What are you working on?

ZEMAN. Accounts.

HODA. Oh.

ZEMAN. Did you need something?

(pause)

Send Nasim in when he gets back.

HODA. Are we rushing into this? What difference would a couple of days make?

ZEMAN. We've already waited too long.

HODA. You'll go easy then?

ZEMAN. Of course.

HODA. Remember she's not a –

ZEMAN. I have to do this my way.

HODA. Sympathy isn't a weakness.

ZEMAN. She'll see the wisdom in time.

HODA. So why not give her some?

ZEMAN. Enough.

(**HODA** *looks down at her hands.*)

It'll be fine. Trust me. This is the best possibility for her.

(**HODA** *nods, but doesn't move.* **ZEMAN** *returns to his work.* **HODA** *looks over his shoulder.*)

HODA. Has Ajani (*Ah-sjon-ee*) paid?

ZEMAN. He's a little behind.

HODA. Again?

ZEMAN. It's to our advantage.

HODA. How?

(*pause*)

You give too much.

ZEMAN. I take care of my family.

HODA. Without Nasim, it'll be much harder…

ZEMAN. I'm not going to lose this job.

HODA. You can't know that.

ZEMAN. I've built a reputation at the plant. They trust me. Respect me. Nasim won't change that.

HODA. But –

ZEMAN. No one's going to find out. When he gets home, send him in.

(**ZEMAN** *returns to his work.*)

HODA. You don't have to be alone in this.

(**HODA** *exits.*)

(**ZEMAN** *continues to work, getting more and more frustrated.*)

(**NASIM** *enters.*)

ZEMAN. You're late.

NASIM. I stopped at the mosque. For prayer.

ZEMAN. With Yasir?

> (**NASIM** *nods, then goes over to his father and takes out another ledger.*)

> I bet his father doesn't have to balance his own accounts.

NASIM. He'd get no help from Yasir.

ZEMAN. Isn't he improving?

NASIM. Not fast enough.

ZEMAN. Too bad.

> (*They work.*)

> Would you take a look at these? I can't seem to…

> (**NASIM** *trades ledgers with* **ZEMAN** *and goes to work.*)

> (**ZEMAN** *stares at* **NASIM**.)

NASIM. What?

ZEMAN. Nothing. It's…nothing.

> (*Looking over* **NASIM**'s *work*)

> Is it that bad?

NASIM. Where's Saratan (*Sarah-tah-n*)? Looks like we're missing a few receipts.

> (**ZEMAN** *goes through another stack of papers.*)

> Oh! And Mama wants more money for cloth next month. Mina hit her growth spurt.

ZEMAN. There's always something. Did Mr. Rafaat ever get you your paycheck?

NASIM. Not yet.

BOTH. I'll talk to him.

NASIM	ZEMAN
I'll see him at work.	There's some business I need to…

NASIM. Business?

ZEMAN. Nothing for you to worry about.

> (**NASIM** *returns to his work.*)

> You've been a great help to me.

(*NASIM doesn't look up.* **ZEMAN** *gets up.*)

You've had this job for a while.

NASIM. Almost three years.

ZEMAN. Three years. Stocking, cleaning, taking inventory must be tiring...tedious anyway. Don't tell me you enjoy it.

NASIM. It's a job. Am I supposed to?

ZEMAN. Wouldn't you like to? I mean...What would you like to do?

NASIM. Finish these accounts.

ZEMAN. In the long run...Do you ever think of...your future? Who you want to...?

NASIM. (*Reprimanding*) Baba!

ZEMAN. All right. Enough. I get it.

(*Finds himself looking at* **NASIM** *again.*)

Such a good worker. Mr. Rafaat'll miss you.

(**NASIM** *looks up from his work.*)

NASIM. Miss me?

ZEMAN. Miss? I meant...

NASIM. Did he fire me?

ZEMAN. No...He's completely pleased with your work.

NASIM. Then what did you – ?

ZEMAN. I...

NASIM. You're sending me to university?

ZEMAN. No!

NASIM. You said that wasn't an option.

ZEMAN. It isn't.

NASIM. Then tell me. What's going – ?

ZEMAN. Things change. It's the way of the world. Seasons, classes, government...people.

NASIM. You're talking like a woman.

ZEMAN. Your mother told me to go easy.

NASIM. Easy?

ZEMAN. It's time for you to take your rightful place in this family, Nasima.

NASIM. Nasim...a?

ZEMAN. (*calling*) Hoda!

(**HODA** *enters with a colorfully wrapped package.*)

(**HODA** *places the gift in* **NASIM**'*s lap and sits next to her.*)

NASIM. What's this for?

HODA. Open it.

(**NASIM** *carefully removes the wrapping paper to reveal a white clothing box.*)

(**NASIM** *takes a floor-length skirt out of the box.*)

NASIMA. (*calling offstage*) Azadeh!

ZEMAN. It's yours.

NASIMA. It's a dress...

ZEMAN. Yes.

NASIMA. I'm at the top of my class.

ZEMAN. You can't...

NASIMA. My studies bring great honor to this –

ZEMAN. They have. Yes.

NASIMA. What will people think if I just disappear? What will you tell the neighbors?

ZEMAN. That Nasim is attending university.

NASIMA. You'd lie?

ZEMAN. We don't have a choice.

NASIMA. Send me there.

ZEMAN. You'd be discovered.

NASIMA. So?

ZEMAN. They'd beat you. And ruin us.

HODA. Zeman!

NASIMA. Would they?

ZEMAN. Who are you to question the law?

NASIMA. What law says that – ?

ZEMAN. I will not lose my daughter because she is too proud to know her place!

NASIMA. You wouldn't let them.

ZEMAN. Don't force me to make that choice.

NASIMA. How is it better if I stay here?

ZEMAN. Our friends understand the practice.

NASIMA. Just let me graduate.

ZEMAN. No.

NASIMA. Why?

ZEMAN. You're my daughter. It's time for you to act like it.

NASIMA. We need my salary.

ZEMAN. We'll manage.

NASIMA. I won't let you do this to me!

HODA. Be still and listen.

NASIMA. I'll listen to sense.

(NASIMA tries to exit.)

ZEMAN. Sit down!

NASIMA. No.

ZEMAN. What did you say?

NASIMA. No.

ZEMAN. This isn't a choice.

NASIMA. I won't do it.

HODA. Don't speak to your father like –

NASIMA. How can you expect me to – ?

ZEMAN. You'll do your duty. Sit down and listen.

NASIMA. But –

ZEMAN. Now.

(NASIMA defiantly returns his gaze.)

(Eventually she relents and sits.)

HODA. You're too pretty. People are starting to notice the change.

NASIMA. Who?

HODA. Nasima!

NASIMA. I am Nasim!

ZEMAN. Not anymore.

NASIMA. I can do so much more…more than a girl.

ZEMAN. Women's work is important.

NASIMA. I'm not going to be someone's slave!

HODA. Is that what you think of me?

NASIMA. Cooking…Cleaning…

HODA. Nasima!

NASIMA. Confined to the house.

ZEMAN. You insolent…

NASIMA. My life, my school, my friends are out there!

ZEMAN. (*Pause*) This was a mistake.

HODA. She needs more time to change her thinking.

NASIMA. I can't change the way I think, who I am.

ZEMAN. We don't have time.

HODA. (*To* **ZEMAN**) Can't you ask for a few more days?

ZEMAN. We've arranged a match.

NASIMA. A match?

HODA. A marriage.

NASIMA. As a woman?

HODA. What else would you…?

NASIMA. I'm to be someone's wife?

ZEMAN. I've spoken to his father.

NASIMA. How could you?

ZEMAN. What?

NASIMA. Barter me away? Sell me. Like cattle!

HODA. Marriage is the greatest blessing for any woman.

ZEMAN. It's a good match.

HODA. And you're of age. What better way is there for you to move on?

NASIMA. I can't marry someone I don't even know!

ZEMAN. I didn't know your mother.

NASIMA. I want more than you.

HODA. How dare – !

NASIMA. You made me your son. Your equal.

HODA. I convinced your father to change you.

ZEMAN. Hoda…

HODA. So when you changed back, you wouldn't have the curse.

NASIMA. The curse? Please. You aren't cursed, Mama.

HODA. Six girls.

NASIMA. How's that a curse?

HODA. I hope you never have to understand.

NASIMA. What is that supposed to mean?

ZEMAN. They wanted me to take another wife.

NASIMA. Who?

ZEMAN. It doesn't matter.

NASIMA. Naneh *(nah-neh)* and Pedar Jan *(ped-er zj-ahn)*? Then I should stay bacha posh *(becca-push)*!

HODA. It's time for you to be a wife.

NASIMA. Sons don't make good wives.

HODA. They make happy families.

NASIMA. We are happy!

ZEMAN. Your mother and sisters have already begun the preparations. They'll teach you how to manage a household.

NASIMA. "None, not even the father or the sovereign can lawfully contract in marriage an adult woman of sound mind without her permission."

ZEMAN. Are you an adult? Well?

NASIMA. Baba…

ZEMAN. Are you?

NASIMA. *(Pause.)* No.

ZEMAN. So I chose.

NASIMA. What about my job?

ZEMAN. Mr. Rafaat will find a replacement.

NASIMA. He'll never be able to replace me.

ZEMAN. Enough daughter!

(This word hits **NASIMA** *harder than any slap could and yet she doesn't turn her face away from her father.)*

NASIMA. At least let me tell him.

(There is another stare off until finally **ZEMAN** *nods.)*

*(**NASIMA** *exits.)*

*(**HODA** *begins to gather up the skirt and its wrappings.)*

*(**ZEMAN** *sinks down to the floor.)*

HODA. That went well.

ZEMAN. That girl…

HODA. If you gave her more time…

ZEMAN. It would just prolong the pain.

HODA. You can't expect her to be content with this. Not without time to process.

ZEMAN. She knew this was coming.

HODA. You're the father of six daughters. Why does her reaction surprise you?

ZEMAN. She's never going to give this up is she?

HODA. You underestimate her. This will make her stronger.

ZEMAN. School is her life.

HODA. She can't deny who she is.

ZEMAN. I was too hard on her. I should…

*(**ZEMAN** *starts to get up.)*

*(**HODA** *stops him with a hand.)*

HODA. No. What she needs now is space.

*(**ZEMAN** *sits back down.)*

Scene Three

(MR. RAFAAT's store the next day)

(NASIMA, in bacha posh, stands behind the counter talking to herself.)

NASIMA. I can't work for you anymore…Something has come up in my family. I can't…

(shakes her head)

Thank you for all that you've done but I have to quit.

(pause)

I'm a girl.

(MR. RAFAAT, the shopkeeper, enters.)

MR. RAFAAT. Day dreaming?

NASIMA. I was just…uh…

(NASIMA turns to straighten the shelves up around her.)

MR. RAFAAT. Once you've finished clowning around, start the inventory.

(NASIMA nods and starts to leave but stops.)

NASIMA. Mr. Rafaat, I…

MR. RAFAAT. Well? What is it?

(The store's bell chimes. YASIR enters.)

(NASIMA runs a hand through her hair and smiles.)

(YASIR walks up to the counter. NASIMA meets him there.)

YASIR. Salam. (*Sal-ah-m*)

NASIMA & MR. RAFAAT. Walaikum as salaam. (*Vall-lay-coom ahs sah-lem*)

MR. RAFAAT. A pleasure as always.

YASIR. My list.

(NASIMA takes YASIR's paper.)

NASIMA. Of course.

YASIR. I can never seem to remember all I need until…

NASIMA. You've remembered you've forgotten it.

YASIR. It's easier to write it all down.

NASIMA. You're always "losing" things. Like the schoolmaster's glasses?

YASIR. You enjoyed seeing him bumble about as much as the rest of us.

NASIMA. No, I –

YASIR. Really.

MR. RAFAAT. (*to* **YASIR**) Here for business or pleasure Mr. Sahar?

NASIMA. I'll get these for you.

(teasing)

Sir.

YASIR. (*teasing back*) Such a fine young worker you have here.

MR. RAFAAT. Il'humdilallah (*Ill-hum-dill-Ah-lah*). How are things at the factory?

YASIR. Fine.

MR. RAFAAT. You should find yourself a good wife.

YASIR. Anyone in mind?

MR. RAFAAT. My cousin has a daughter. Mehran (*Meh-r-ah-n*)? You know her?

YASIR. Yeah, but…I don't know…

(**NASIMA** *coughs and casts* **YASIR** *a suggestive/knowing glance.*)

(**YASIR** *brushes it off.*)

MR. RAFAAT. A man shouldn't wait too long.

NASIMA. Here are your groceries. Sir.

YASIR. Right. Thank you.

MR. RAFAAT. I could talk to your father.

YASIR. That's very kind. I'm sure he's considering every option.

(to NASIMA*)*

How much?

NASIMA. 1,240 Afghani.

MR. RAFAAT. She's very...pretty. And children! She wants lots of children.

*(*YASIR *hands her the money.* NASIMA *gives him change.)*

YASIR. Until next week.

*(*YASIR *exits.* NASIMA *stares after him.)*

MR. RAFAAT. The inventory?

*(*NASIMA *makes her way to the back.)*

(She stops when she sees ZEMAN *through the store window.)*

(She turns back.)

NASIMA. Mr. Rafaat?

MR. RAFAAT. What now?

NASIMA. I can't work for you anymore.

MR. RAFAAT. You can't quit.

NASIMA. Thank you for your charity and kindness.

*(*NASIMA *removes her apron and hands it to* MR. RAFAAT*.)*

*(*ZEMAN *enters.)*

MR. RAFAAT. *(to* ZEMAN*)* This your doing?

*(*NASIMA *brushes by* ZEMAN*.)*

He's my only clerk!

(pause)

Nasim's a great worker. A credit to you.

ZEMAN. Then why are you so slow to pay him?

MR. RAFAAT. I could've sworn...

*(*ZEMAN *takes a step closer.)*

It was an oversight.

ZEMAN. Three months in a row?

MR. RAFAAT. I always got it to you.

ZEMAN. Late. A few weeks make all of the difference.

MR. RAFAAT. Is this any way to treat a friend?

ZEMAN. I came to ask you the same question.

MR. RAFAAT. So this spectacle's meant to teach me a lesson?
It's an interesting way to demand a raise.

ZEMAN. It's overdue.

MR. RAFAAT. You'll need to give me some time.

ZEMAN. I don't have any to give!

MR. RAFAAT. Money is tight right now. I can't –

ZEMAN. Don't you think I know?

MR. RAFAAT. But demanding a raise?

ZEMAN. Or recompense…

MR. RAFAAT. What?

ZEMAN. Nasim is bacha posh.

MR. RAFAAT. Bacha…

ZEMAN. It's time for her to…

MR. RAFAAT. A bacha posh? In my shop?

ZEMAN. I have another daughter just as capable as Nasim.
Perhaps better.

MR. RAFAAT. You want me to hire another?

ZEMAN. Yes.

MR. RAFAAT. You're insane.

(MR. RAFAAT *turns to leave.* ZEMAN *steps in his way.*)

ZEMAN. I wonder what your other customers will think
when they hear how forgetful you are with your debts.

(MR. RAFAAT *stops.*)

MR. RAFAAT. I never pictured you as one to…

ZEMAN. I can keep a secret if you can.

(*Slowly,* MR. RAFAAT *sits back down.*)

MR. RAFAAT. How's her math?

ZEMAN. Adequate.

MR. RAFAAT. Nasim's was impeccable.

ZEMAN. Not at first.

(He knows **ZEMAN** *speaks the truth.)*

MR. RAFAAT. I won't trade down.

ZEMAN. Nasim will train her at home. She's quick to learn.

MR. RAFAAT. I don't know…

ZEMAN. About Nasim's paycheck…

*(***ZEMAN** *mimes pulling a slip of paper out of his pocket.)*

Is this it?

MR. RAFAAT. What…? Oh!

(pause)

It's a lot to ask of…

ZEMAN. It's my final offer.

MR. RAFAAT. A bacha posh.

*(***ZEMAN** *sighs and mimes pulling another piece of paper
from his pocket.)*

ZEMAN. What's this? How kind of you to pay a month in
advance!

MR. RAFAAT. Well…I don't see how it could hurt.

*(***ZEMAN** *hands* **MR. RAFAAT** *the papers.)*

*(***MR. RAFAAT** *mimes ripping them up.)*

ZEMAN. Thank you.

(They shake hands.)

Scene Four

(YASIR's house. YASIR plays with a soccer ball. NASIMA enters.)

YASIR. Aren't you supposed to be working? What happened? Did I get you in trouble?

NASIMA. My family needs me somewhere else.

YASIR. Got another job?

NASIMA. Of sorts.

YASIR. What does that mean?

NASIMA. I can't tell you.

YASIR. Why?

NASIMA. Would you just stop?

(YASIR rolls his eyes and steps away.)

(NASIM rests a reassuring hand on YASIR's arm.)

NASIMA. It's family stuff. Honor. I can't…
YASIR. Oh.

(NASIM quickly takes back her hand and turns away.)

(YASIR shakes his head.)

NASIMA. I'm sorry.

YASIR. It's okay. I get it.

NASIMA. Right.

YASIR. At least you won't have to deal with Mr. Rafaat anymore.

NASIMA. Can I talk to your sister?

YASIR. Which one?

NASIMA. You know…

YASIR. Why do you want to talk to her?

NASIMA. Please.

(YASIR studies NASIMA, finally deciding it's okay.)

YASIR. (calling) Laila!

(to NASIMA)

I don't know why you have to be so mysterious…Have your father talk to mine. Propose already.

(NASIMA *punches* YASIR *in the arm.* YASIR *rubs it. Calling again:*)

Lai…

(LAILA *enters.*)

You have a visitor.

(YASIR *sits down on the stoop.*)

(LAILA *pulls her veil more over her face.*)

NASIMA. (*to* YASIR) Don't you need to do something?

YASIR. I can't leave you.

NASIMA. How am I supposed to…? You know.

YASIR. That's the point.

NASIMA. Can you at least…?

(YASIR *moves away from them.*)

A little more.

(*again*)

More…

(*again*)

Keep going.

(YASIR *bumps into the house.*)

YASIR. Want me to cover my ears too?

NASIMA. That'd be nice.

YASIR. I'm watching you.

(YASIR *pulls an MP3 player out of his pocket and plugs the headphones into his ears.*)

(LAILA *and* NASIMA *talk trying to make it look like a casual conversation.*)

LAILA. He's fine.

NASIMA. They told me today.

LAILA. It's about time.

NASIMA. No warning.

LAILA. Did you need one?

NASIMA. I was hoping I could finish school.

LAILA. You couldn't last another year.

NASIMA. Why not?

LAILA. We're not all blind. You can resume your place.

NASIMA. As what?

LAILA. My friend.

NASIMA. I am your friend.

LAILA. But we can't talk. You're always with Yasir, or working, or running errands, or…

NASIMA. I had to.

LAILA. Well, try to think of the positives.

NASIMA. Like what?

LAILA. You won't have to look so frumpy all of the time.

NASIMA. Are you familiar with the burqa?

LAILA. You're the strangest girl I've ever met.

NASIMA. Boy.

LAILA. Bacha posh.

NASIMA. Same thing.

LAILA. You're not like any boy I've ever seen.

NASIMA. (*glancing over at* **YASIR**) I've fooled Yasir.

LAILA. Guys don't notice anything.

NASIMA. Then why do I have to change?

LAILA. They will notice…Your body.

NASIMA. He didn't. Did he? What did he say?

LAILA. You do like him!

NASIMA. He's my best friend.

LAILA. He's also a boy. You can't hide it from me.

NASIMA. It doesn't matter anyway. He thinks I'm…and I'm engaged.

(**LAILA** *tries to hug* **NASIMA,** *but catches herself.*)

LAILA. Azadeh must be so jealous.

NASIMA. I can't be a wife!

LAILA. You can't be a husband either, Nasima.

NASIMA. Don't call me that!

LAILA. You better get used to it.

(NASIMA *gags.*)

All girls have to go sometime.

NASIMA. Why haven't you?

LAILA. Bacha posh always get married right away. It's the way it's done.

NASIMA. Don't you want to get married?

LAILA. Of course.

NASIMA. But…?

LAILA. There hasn't been a proposal.

(NASIM *looks at her skeptically.*)

From the right man.

NASIMA. You have a say?

LAILA. Father doesn't think so but…

NASIMA. Who is he? Your man.

LAILA. No one.

NASIMA. Come on. You can tell me.

LAILA. No.

NASIMA. Please!

LAILA. I haven't met him yet.

NASIMA. Right…But there have been others?

LAILA. I don't want to talk about it.

NASIMA. How'd you get rid of them?

LAILA. My father wants to see me happy.

NASIMA. And mine doesn't?

LAILA. Maybe he shows love differently.

NASIMA. How did you do it? Come on!

LAILA. There's nothing you can do about it now.

NASIMA. Thanks a lot.

LAILA. Maybe you'll like him.

NASIMA. And maybe I won't.

LAILA. It won't hurt to try.

NASIMA. So you'd subject yourself for the right man?

LAILA. Wouldn't you?

NASIMA. I thought you'd be on my side.

(*LAILA rests a hand on NASIMA's arm.*)

LAILA. Don't forget yourself.

NASIMA. I'm trying not to.

LAILA. Are you?

(*YASIR turns around.*)

YASIR. Go inside.

(*LAILA takes back her hand as if burned.*)

(*YASIR steps between NASIMA and LAILA.*)

LAILA. But, I –

YASIR. Now.

(*She hesitates then exits.*)

(*YASIR shoves NASIMA.*)

Think you can take advantage of me?

(*Shoves again*)

Huh?

NASIMA. (*Ducking away*) It's not what it looks like…

(*YASIR grabs NASIMA by her shirt collar.*)

YASIR. Leave my sister alone.

NASIMA. I brushed her hand.

YASIR. That's all?

NASIMA. You saw the whole thing.

YASIR. Did I?

NASIMA. (*Pushing YASIR off*) Yes.

(*YASIR rushes NASIMA, knocking her down, and pinning her to the ground.*)

(He sits on top of her.)

Don't tell your father!

YASIR. What did you say to her?

NASIMA. What?

YASIR. I'm responsible for anything that –

NASIMA. Nothing happened.

YASIR. Her honor. My whole family's!

NASIMA. I'm getting married.

YASIR. *(sitting up)* Married?

NASIMA. I didn't know how to tell you.

YASIR. You're serious?

NASIMA. Yeah.

YASIR. I'm…Me too.

NASIMA. What?

YASIR. Both of us? That's crazy!

NASIMA. Are you excited?

YASIR. Does Laila know about this?

NASIMA. Laila?

YASIR. Wait! That's why you were holding hands!

NASIMA. We weren't…

YASIR. It's her isn't it?

NASIMA. Laila?

YASIR. Welcome to the family!

(YASIR embraces NASIMA who tries to shield herself.)

(NASIMA pushes off a confused YASIR.)

(They turn away from each other.)

NASIMA. It's arranged. How could I…?

YASIR. Right.

NASIMA. They just told me about it this morning.

YASIR. Well, it could be Laila. Couldn't it?

NASIMA. Doubt it.

(pause.)

What if we refuse?

YASIR. What?

NASIMA. We can refuse!

YASIR. Can we?

NASIMA. Why not?

YASIR. But marriage is a blessing.

NASIMA. You sound like my father. It's our life. Why do we have to be married now?

YASIR. Family honor. Remember?

NASIMA. Shouldn't we have a say in our futures?

YASIR. Yeah. We'll say we aren't going to marry and you're coming to university with me.

NASIMA. That'll go over well.

YASIR. It was your idea.

NASIMA. I didn't mean we'd…

YASIR. Then why bring it up?

NASIMA. They can't stop me from dreaming.

YASIR. Coward.

NASIMA. I know my place.

YASIR. But if both of us…

NASIMA. We can't.

YASIR. You think you're the only one. Get through school, marry, take over the factory. Yeah it's a dream come true.

NASIMA. You poor soul.

YASIR. I'm not ready to be married! Look at me! I can't care for someone else…you know…like that.

NASIMA. Yasir, the romantic.

YASIR. No! I mean…I don't know how to keep a wife.

NASIMA. Keep?

YASIR. You know what I mean. Protecting, providing…?

NASIMA. Responsibility's not your strong suit.

YASIR. Not helping.

NASIMA. What's there to know anyway? She'll never ask for anything and wait on you hand and foot.

YASIR. Isn't marriage more than that? I want a family. Maybe not now, but I want to come home to someone who's mine.

NASIMA. Yours.

YASIR. Who cares for me. You know? It doesn't hurt that it's a commandment.

NASIMA. What do you want her to be like?

YASIR. What do you mean?

NASIMA. What type of person…? What are you going to talk about?

YASIR. I don't know.

NASIMA. You're spending the rest of your life with her!

YASIR. Talking's what I have you for.

NASIMA. I won't be there.

YASIR. What? Where are you going?

NASIMA. We can't hang out anymore.

(YASIR *laughs.*)

I'm serious.

YASIR. Why?

NASIMA. My father doesn't want me wasting time, you know, with football and stuff.

YASIR. He can't do that!

NASIMA. He already has.

(NASIMA *starts to go.*)

(*She runs back and hugs* YASIR, *but eventually pulls away.*)

Goodbye.

(NASIMA *exits.* YASIR *watches her go.*)

Scene Five

(NASIMA's House. AZADEH, 15, NASIMA's younger sister, holds out a shirt for NASIMA.)

AZADEH. Arms up.

(Reluctantly, NASIMA lifts her arms.)

You have to take your shirt off first.

(NASIMA rips off her shirt, throwing it on the floor.)

(She stands in her undershirt, glaring at AZADEH.)

(AZADEH stares at her.)

(Finally, NASIMA sticks her arms out.)

(AZADEH slips the shirt over her head.)

(It gets stuck. AZADEH tries to pull it down.)

NASIMA. Get me out of here!

AZADEH. Stop! You'll rip it! Just…Would you – ? Quit moving!

(NASIMA stops. AZADEH pulls the shirt down.)

There.

NASIMA. Great.

AZADEH. Now the skirt.

NASIMA. Skirt?

AZADEH. You can't wear pants.

NASIMA. Why not?

AZADEH. Come on.

(AZADEH holds it out to her.)

(NASIMA looks around to see a way out. She can't see one.)

(She steps into the skirt.)

(NASIMA's stance is too wide for a girl. She attempts to walk.)

(**AZADEH** *laughs.*)

(**NASIMA** *turns back, glaring at* **AZADEH**.)

(**AZADEH** *holds a headscarf in her hands.*)

Here.

NASIMA. What am I supposed to do with this?

AZADEH. Just watch. Are you watching?

NASIMA. Yes!

(**AZADEH** *lays the headscarf on her head.*)

AZADEH. So you take this side and place it there. And then…you take this piece and place it here…

(**AZADEH** *rapidly and artfully folds the head covering into place.*)

And then, like so and…it's done!

(**AZADEH** *turns to see* **NASIMA** *tangled in her headscarf.*)

Nasima!

NASIMA. What?

AZADEH. I'll show you again. Watch.

(**NASIMA** *watches as* **AZADEH** *quickly folds the head scarf into place.*)

NASIMA. Of course! Why didn't I get it before?

AZADEH. You're not even trying!

NASIMA. Fine.

(**NASIMA** *takes her scarf and attempts to recreate* **AZADEH**'s *movements.*)

(*She fails miserably.* **AZADEH** *laughs.*)

It wouldn't be so easy for you either.

(**AZADEH** *lowers her gaze.*)

AZADEH. Be patient with yourself.

NASIMA. You go so fast I can't even tell what you're doing.

AZADEH. I'll slow down.

NASIMA. Who needs this anyway?

AZADEH. We take the scarf to show our devotion to Allah, to His word, to His prophet. It's a symbol.

NASIMA. Why don't men have to tie table cloths on their heads?

AZADEH. Just try.

(**NASIMA** *snatches the scarf from her sister and tries again.*)

(*picking up the pattern*) Have you seen the pattern for your wedding dress?

(**AZADEH** *holds out the paper for* **NASIMA,** *who makes an ambiguous noise as she unties her failed attempt at the headscarf.*)

Mama and I must have been working on it for a month already.

NASIMA. A month?

AZADEH. At least…

NASIMA. Why didn't you tell me earlier?

AZADEH. We thought you'd realize…

NASIMA. That you had plans for me to be a wife?

AZADEH. Isn't that how it works? Come on. Every girl dreams of her wedding…

NASIMA. I'm not a girl.

(**AZADEH** *sighs and puts down the pattern and picks up some intricate embroidery.* **NASIMA** *goes back to tying her scarf, failing more and more miserably each time.*)

AZADEH. Your fiancé must be rich. I've never seen fabric like he sent. Shukria *(Shoo-cree-ah)* and Zahra's *(Zah-rah)* dresses weren't half as nice as yours is going to be. Their fiancés sent nice things, but…Has Mama showed you all of the stuff? Maybe she'll show it to you later. You should ask. I mean, if we have time. You have so much to learn. I hope that I get to have such nice things when I get married. I can't wait to find out who…

(**NASIMA** *fails and throws the headscarf on the floor.*)

NASIMA. Would you be quiet? I'm trying to concentrate!

AZADEH. You can do it.

NASIMA. Leave me alone. I don't need your help.

AZADEH. I...I'll go see what Mama is doing.

> (**AZADEH** *exits.*)

> (**NASIMA** *finds the scarf, places it on her head and looking in the mirror slowly tries again.*)

> (*This time she succeeds.*)

> (*She stands up to get the full effect from all angles.*)

> (*She smooths her clothes down her curves. Uncomfortably, she crosses her arms and sits back down.*)

NASIMA. Nasima.

> (*pause, looking up*)

Help me.

Scene Six

(NASIMA's house. HODA is teaching NASIMA how to cook. AZADEH prepares clothes and other items for NASIMA's marriage.)

HODA. Not so much now. Gently.

(a knock)

(pushing in on NASIMA's back) Stand up straight. No man wants a cripple.

(AZADEH opens the door for LAILA.)

AZADEH. *(hugging her)* Laila!

NASIMA. *(Jumping away from the stove)* What are you doing here?

LAILA. Thought you might need some help with the wedding.

NASIMA. How's Yasir?

AZADEH. Who?

LAILA. My brother.

NASIMA & HODA. Her brother.

NASIMA. Don't they need you to help with…?

LAILA. They'll never miss me. It's a zoo. My sisters and aunts are so excited I can hardly stand to be around them. It's always "we need this for the wedding" and "we need that for the wedding!"

NASIMA. So you came here to escape?

LAILA. Bad choice, right?

AZADEH. Must be nice to have so much help.

HODA. If they need anything…let us know.

LAILA. Thank you. I will.

HODA. Can I get you some tea?

LAILA. Thank you.

(to NASIM)

The skirt suits you.

NASIMA. Don't start.

(**HODA** *hands a cup to* **LAILA**.)

LAILA. Really! I think it's nice.

HODA. (*to* **NASIMA**) Is that any way to receive a compliment?

NASIMA. (*taking* **LAILA**'s *face in her hands*) Thank you.

(*kissing her cheek*)

Thank you.

(*kissing her other cheek*)

Thank you.

LAILA. It's true.

(**NASIMA** *grimaces and her mother scowls at her. They return to their work.* **LAILA** *sits down next to* **AZADEH**.)

How's she doing?

HODA. Fighting every step of the way.

NASIMA. Am not.

AZADEH. We've been working nonstop making the gifts and food. The worst part is she needs everything new.

HODA. We probably should have started sooner.

LAILA. Well, it's nice to have another set of hands to help out around here.

HODA. (*to* **NASIMA**) Feet together. A woman does not slouch.

(**NASIMA** *adjusts.*)

AZADEH. She's a fast learner.

HODA. (*tasting*) We'll make a wife out of her yet.

AZADEH. We haven't had a wedding in ages! Not since Zahra and that was almost two years ago! I can't wait for my turn.

LAILA. Don't worry. It'll come.

AZADEH. What do you think it'll be like?

HODA. You're letting it boil over.

(**NASIMA** *removes the pot. She tries to put it on the counter.*)

Not there. It's hot.

(**NASIMA** *turns to take it to the table.*)

No!

NASIMA. Then where?

HODA. Is that any way to ask…?

NASIMA. Mama!

HODA. (*guiding*) Will you please…?

NASIMA. Help me.

(**HODA** *looks at her disapprovingly.*)

Mama…will you please…help me?

(**HODA** *opens the drawer and pulls out a wooden trivet which she places on the table.* **NASIMA** *turns around again, taking the pot to the table.*)

(*Her legs become tangled in her skirt.*)

(*She trips, almost dropping the pot.*)

(**NASIMA** *slams the pot down on the table.*)

This stupid skirt!

HODA. Hush!

NASIMA. I can't walk in this thing!

HODA. Quiet!

NASIMA. How can I work if I can't move?

HODA. Hold your tongue or I'll have to make you.

NASIMA. You wouldn't. Not to me.

HODA. It isn't our place to question.

NASIMA. Why?

HODA. You're a woman.

NASIMA. I'll get Baba.

AZADEH. No.

HODA. Go ahead.

NASIMA. Fine.

(**NASIMA** *stops when she sees herself in a mirror.*)

HODA. Get the cloth from the bedroom. We'll work on that next.

*(**NASIMA** exits. **HODA** sits down.)*

LAILA. She'll adjust.

AZADEH. She's much better than yesterday.

HODA. I don't know what I'm going to do with that girl. She's going to kill us all.

LAILA. Or her husband.

*(**HODA** and **LAILA** exchange a look.)*

*(**NASIMA** returns with the cloth.)*

(She plops down and attempts to thread her needle, holding the thread steady and jabbing the needle at it.)

AZADEH. Can I...?

NASIMA. I can do it.

HODA. Let your sister help.

*(**NASIMA** groans.)*

*(**AZADEH** runs over and tries to edge her way in.)*

*(**NASIMA** avoids her.)*

AZADEH. Did you lick it?

NASIMA. Of course I licked it!

AZADEH. Well try it again.

NASIMA. I don't have to –

*(**AZADEH** reaches for the thread.)*

*(**NASIMA** pulls it away licking it several times.)*

It doesn't help!

HODA. *(gesturing for the needle)* Here.

*(**NASIMA** hands it over.)*

*(**HODA** threads it without difficulty and hands it to **NASIMA**.)*

*(**NASIMA** begins sewing. The group watches her.)*

NASIMA. What?

AZADEH. You have to keep the needle steady.

(NASIMA tries again.)

Here. Let me.

(The girls scuffle.)

HODA. Girls! Here.

(She separates them.)

AZADEH. It's crooked.

NASIMA. Mind your own –

AZADEH. It is. You're just going to have to redo it.

HODA. Let me see.

NASIMA. I was doing fine.

(NASIMA hands the garment to HODA who rips out the crooked seam.)

NASIMA. Mama!

HODA. Straight. Like this.

(She sews a little bit and hands it back to NASIMA.)

AZADEH. Told you.

(NASIMA sticks AZADEH with her needle. AZADEH shrieks.)

HODA. Azadeh!

(AZADEH returns to her work.)

LAILA. I hear Mr. Kohistani is going back to school.

NASIMA. What for?

LAILA. Wants to get his master's.

HODA. He's a smart man. You were lucky to have him.

NASIMA. Who told you?

LAILA. You know. I heard it around.

HODA. I heard it's actually because he's looking to get married. He wants to improve his opportunities.

NASIMA. Whatever.

LAILA. A lot of girls want a smart one.

AZADEH. Is he handsome? Do you like him?

LAILA. Me?

NASIMA. A smart man, fairly attractive, progressive thinker...Sounds like your type.

AZADEH. It's like a fairy tale. Poor school master and factory princess fall in love!

LAILA. I wouldn't go that far...

NASIMA. (*teasing*) Oh, Mr. Kohistani, what beautiful eyes you have! How dare you deprive the world by hiding behind your glasses?

LAILA. I don't even know him!

HODA. All right girls....

(**HODA** *exits. They return to working.*)

NASIMA. (*lowering her voice*) Who's Yasir marrying?

LAILA. He misses you.

NASIMA. Tell me.

LAILA. He's looking all over for you.

NASIMA. Really?

LAILA. He's kind of...frantic.

NASIMA. Serves him right.

AZADEH. Do you like him?

LAILA. Yes she does.   **NASIMA.** What? No.

AZADEH. Okay...

LAILA. Tell her.

NASIMA. I don't like him!

AZADEH. Does he know you're getting married?

NASIMA. Kind of.

LAILA. He thinks she's marrying a woman.

AZADEH. No!

NASIMA. I couldn't bear for him to see me like this.

LAILA. He'd never recognize you.

NASIMA. Right? Imagine how this would improve my football. He didn't think anything could make me any worse!

(They laugh.)

*(**NASIMA** realized that she has sewn what she's been working on to her skirt. She moves away slowly, carefully, trying to hide it.)*

AZADEH. *(pulling* **LAILA** *aside, whispering)* What do you think you are doing?

LAILA. You can't expect her to change overnight.

AZADEH. It doesn't help her to think about what she can't have.

*(They see **NASIMA**. She rips out the seam. **LAILA** bursts into laughter.)*

What?

LAILA. She…She sewed…

*(**AZADEH** sees. She joins in laughing.)*

NASIMA. I can hear you.

(The laughter dies down.)

LAILA. So…What's next?

AZADEH. Embroidery?

LAILA. She'll love that.

*(**AZADEH** exits to get the scarves.)*

NASIMA. A couple of weeks ago I was learning integral calculus. Now I decorate oversized handkerchiefs.

LAILA. You're moving up in life.

AZADEH. Can't get married without new clothes.

NASIMA. What a waste.

LAILA. Careful. We don't want you to sew it to your head.

*(**NASIMA** sticks out her tongue at **LAILA**.)*

AZADEH. Why do you want to run around with smelly boys anyway?

NASIMA. You should try it sometime. Maybe you'd like it.

AZADEH. No thank you. You'd always come home beat up.

NASIMA. Would not!

LAILA. Why do boys fight all the time?

AZADEH. Yeah!

LAILA. Can't they just discuss things like…?

NASIMA. Women? I don't expect you two to understand.

LAILA. You did.

NASIMA. That's different.

LAILA. How?

AZADEH. The world would be a much nicer place if women were in charge.

LAILA. It would.

NASIMA. Yeah…We'd all sit around and sew all day.

LAILA. You mean you wouldn't like that?

(NASIMA *scowls.* LAILA *and* AZADEH *laugh.*)

(HODA *enters. She checks the pot on the stove.*)

HODA. Are you getting anything done over here?

NASIMA. Do we ever?

HODA. Excuse me?

LAILA. What's that supposed to mean?

NASIMA. Talk. That's all we ever do. Sew and talk. If I had an afghani for every piece of gossip I've heard today alone…

HODA. Nasima!

LAILA. That's of more substance than all that's spoken between men.

NASIMA. Nothing ever comes of it.

AZADEH. Men talking?

NASIMA. Women!

LAILA. I wouldn't stake my life on that. They never expect ideas to come from us. That's what makes it so fun.

NASIMA. So that's why they lock us up.

HODA. A woman's place is in the home.

AZADEH. They don't lock us…

NASIMA. What do you call it?

AZADEH. Love…they…

NASIMA. Love. Really.

AZADEH. Men can't do what we can.

NASIMA. You mean they won't! They don't want to.

LAILA. She means…

AZADEH. You know…Children.

HODA. Azadeh!

NASIMA. Working doesn't inhibit that. Look at the west.

HODA. It's our duty to Allah. You must respect His gift.

NASIMA. Allah created me. He allowed me to be a man.

HODA. Bacha posh.

LAILA. Allah allows us to choose.

NASIMA. But he determines our fate. Would he let me go this long if He didn't think – ?

LAILA. He allows sinners to sin.

(pause)

NASIMA. I live for knowledge. Not housework. Is that a sin?

LAILA. Why can't you have both?

AZADEH. You've been able to balance it well enough so far.

NASIMA. But soon I'll have a husband who'll expect…

(The girls let their gaze fall back to their work.)

HODA. What?

NASIMA. A housekeeper. Not a scholar. Not me.

HODA. Marriage is a lesson in sacrifice.

NASIMA. Only for us. For women.

LAILA. Who says he'll be like that? Not all men are.

NASIMA. Really?

LAILA. You should know. You were one.

NASIMA. But there's a huge chance that he'll be –

LAILA. And a chance that he won't.

HODA. Don't you trust us to make sure he's –

NASIMA. Who is he?

HODA. A very nice young man.

NASIMA. Young? Do I know him?

HODA. You will.

NASIMA. Tell me. Please.

> (**HODA** *returns to her work.*)

> How do you know he's so good? Have you even met him?

HODA. Your father and I chose him for you.

NASIMA. I can make my own decisions. I've had freedom. I know how to use it.

HODA. To accept your place?

NASIMA. You've never wanted what men have?

> (**NASIMA** *looks into each woman's eyes in turn.* **LAILA** *looks away.*)

AZADEH. We're free too.

HODA. This is not a choice.

NASIMA. It should be.

HODA. You've been given a gift. To live both lives. Now you get to be married. Have a family.

AZADEH. You have everything.

NASIMA. Had.

AZADEH. You're acting like a selfish –

HODA. Azadeh. Don't.

NASIMA. Do you want to finish that sentence?

AZADEH. You're ungrateful. If I could have –

NASIMA. Take it. Talk to Baba. I'm sure he'll be able to work something out.

> (*silence*)

> What? You scared?

AZADEH. Be quiet.

HODA. (*to* **NASIMA.**) Please.

(**NASIMA** *sighs and picks up her work again.*)

LAILA. (*To* **NASIMA**) You'll find a way to make it work. We all do.

NASIMA. I want to live. Not just "make it work."

LAILA. It was a poor choice of words.

NASIMA. It's no way to live.

AZADEH. The men are trying to follow the laws, to respect us.

NASIMA. Then why don't they?

AZADEH. Why won't you let them?

NASIMA. They're weak. Weak, weak, weak. Can't they stand a little temptation?

(**NASIMA** *plays flirtatiously with her headscarf.*)

(**LAILA** *laughs. She clamps her hand over her mouth.*)

HODA. That's quite enough.

AZADEH. We're helping them to…

(**NASIMA** *removes the scarf seductively.*)

Stop it.

NASIMA. That's so much better.

(**NASIMA** *dangles the scarf in* **AZADEH**'s *face.* **HODA** *snatches it from her.*)

HODA. Where is your respect?

NASIMA. Respect? That's a funny word for imprisonment.

(**HODA** *slaps* **NASIMA.**)

HODA. You may question me or your father, but Allah? There is a divine order given to us. That demands respect.

(*pause*)

Excuse me.

(*She exits.* **NASIMA** *sinks to the floor.*)

AZADEH. Happy?

NASIMA. I didn't want this!

LAILA. "Allah curses those men who make themselves resemble women or those women who make themselves resemble men." The Prophet. Praised be his name.

NASIMA. I didn't do this…They did…

(LAILA *goes over to embrace* NASIMA.)

LAILA. You get to choose now. He's giving you a second chance.

(AZADEH *puts down her work, joining them.*)

AZADEH. I pray your husband's a good man.

Scene Seven

(YASIR's house. LAILA reads a book. YASIR enters with a cloth in hand. He drops it on her book. LAILA removes the cloth from her lap.)

LAILA. What's this?

YASIR. It was on the list.

LAILA. No, I mean, why pink?

YASIR. What's wrong with it?

(LAILA holds it up to her face.)

LAILA. What do you think?

YASIR. Looks fine to me.

(LAILA places the cloth on his head.)

LAILA. Then you wear it.

YASIR. You should have been more specific.

(YASIR leans back, defeated, on the couch.)

LAILA. What's wrong?

(YASIR pulls the scarf off of his head.)

YASIR. Nothing.

LAILA. I'm sure he's fine.

YASIR. Where could he be? A man shouldn't have to get married without the help of his best friend!

LAILA. You have us.

YASIR. That's different.

LAILA. Right.

(pause)

I'm sure Nasim's feeling the same way.

YASIR. I'm sorry.

LAILA. Why?

YASIR. Must be hard for you. With the way you two...you know...

LAILA. What?

YASIR. Don't play games with me! You like him.

LAILA. He's your best friend.

YASIR. So?

LAILA. I couldn't like him. He's like a sis – brother. I can't believe you thought that we...

YASIR. He's getting married.

LAILA. He told you?

YASIR. You know?

LAILA. Did he tell you who...?

YASIR. Not completely, but...

LAILA. Then you know. That he isn't...

YASIR. Marrying you?

LAILA. Me?

YASIR. Drop the act. You obviously like him.

LAILA. No, I don't. Really.

YASIR. Could've fooled me.

LAILA. Stop.

YASIR. Wish he was...marrying you.

(pause)

LAILA. Did you tell him about your engagement?

YASIR. Of course.

*(**LAILA** smiles and takes out her book again. **YASIR** sits up.)*

I know you know.

*(**LAILA** ignores him. He begins to poke her.)*

Come on. Tell me who she is.

LAILA. Stop it!

*(**YASIR** begins to tickle her until **LAILA** laughs uncontrollably.)*

YASIR. I'm wearing you down.

LAILA. I don't know what you're talking about.

(She falls to the ground. She holds her book up as a shield.)

(YASIR *snatches it from her.)*

Give it back.

YASIR. Not until you tell me.

*(**LAILA** grabs for the book.)*

(YASIR *side steps, constantly keeping the book out of her reach.)*

*(**LAILA** gives up, picking up the forgotten cloth.)*

LAILA. What do you want to know?

YASIR. Her name.

LAILA. I can't tell you that.

YASIR. Well then…what's she like?

LAILA. She's fifty and covered in warts. It's true. I've seen her.

YASIR. And father chose her because…?

LAILA. She happens to be a fabulous cook and fairly wealthy.

YASIR. Thank goodness.

*(**LAILA** grabs her book.)*

LAILA. You'll be very happy.

Scene Eight

(AZADEH stands in front of a mirror. She wears no headscarf and her hair is short. She is bacha posh.)

HODA. It's only for a little while. Just until the need passes.

AZADEH. I don't know what I'm supposed to do!

HODA. Nasima will help you.

AZADEH. She'll kill me.

HODA. She understands our situation.

AZADEH. Let me marry! Nasima can…

HODA. When it's right, we will find you a wonderful match.

AZADEH. I'm ready now.

HODA. You have to wait.

AZADEH. I always have to wait.

HODA. And you still haven't learned the lesson. Patience.

AZADEH. I have. I'm just tired of always having to be. I want things too, Mama.

HODA. (*resting a hand on* AZADEH's *shoulder*) It will come. You're a good girl.

(AZADEH pulls away.)

AZADEH. Patience. Right.

(HODA cautiously pulls AZADEH into an embrace.)

(NASIMA enters.)

(She stops abruptly as she sees AZADEH.)

NASIMA. What's going on?

HODA. Come here, let's get you dressed for the engagement party.

(NASIMA approaches AZADEH who can't meet her gaze.)

NASIMA. You wanted this all along!

HODA. (*Pulling* NASIMA *away*) Control your temper.

NASIMA. How could you? Look at me!

(AZADEH can't.)

AZADEH. I didn't...I don't...

NASIMA. All the time, acting like you wanted this, when you were just waiting it out. How long have you known?

AZADEH. They told me I couldn't –

NASIMA. When did they tell you? When?

AZADEH. Yesterday.

NASIMA. Liar.

AZADEH. Why would I lie?

NASIMA. I trusted you.

HODA. Nasima!

NASIMA. (*turning to* **HODA**) And you...you knew this would have to happen. The family would suffer without Nasim and we just couldn't have that!

AZADEH. I didn't ask for this.   **HODA.** No. We couldn't.

(**HODA** *holds out the dress to* **NASIMA**.)

HODA. Now please.

(**NASIMA** *looks at the aftermath of her actions.*)

(**NASIMA** *takes the dress and hurls it across the room.*)

NASIMA. We're not your dolls to dress up and do with as you please.

HODA. We can't make it without your salary.

NASIMA. So have me work. Keep me bacha posh. Don't do this to her.

HODA. That isn't what we're trying to do.

NASIMA. Then what is it?

HODA. You need to move on.

(*Offering the dress to* **NASIMA**)

Get dressed.

(*A moment.* **NASIMA** *takes it.*)

(**AZADEH** *looks down at the floor as* **HODA** *exits.*)

(*Slowly,* **NASIMA** *steps into the dress.*)

(*She gets it on but can't fasten the back.*)

NASIMA. (*reaching*) Would you...? Please.

    (**AZADEH** *snaps back to reality.*)

    (*She goes over to* **NASIMA** *and fastens the dress.*)

AZADEH. There.

    (**AZADEH** *sinks down to her seat.*)

    (**NASIMA** *strokes her hair.*)

NASIMA. Your beautiful hair.

    (**AZADEH** *embraces* **NASIMA**.)

AZADEH. I promise...I didn't want to...

NASIMA. I know...It'll grow back. Short hair is much nicer anyway. You don't have to spend as much time washing it.

AZADEH. But...

NASIMA. When it grows back it will be thicker and even more beautiful.

AZADEH. It feels so...different.

NASIMA. Lighter? I remember when Mama cut mine...Felt like I was flying.

AZADEH. Zahra told me you ran all around the house flapping your arms, until...

NASIMA. I was five.

AZADEH. ...you broke Mama's vase.

NASIMA. Someday I'll get her a new one.

AZADEH. She still has the pieces. I can't do this.

NASIMA. You can.

AZADEH. I don't know how to act or work or...

NASIMA. For Mr. Rafaat? You'll have to take inventory. It's just counting, nothing horrible. Making change is worse. But you'll get the hang of it...Talk to the customers. Smile. You won't have a problem with that. And...don't be late. Ever. He never forgives you. Think of all the suitors you'll have waiting, wanting a bacha posh.

AZADEH. I'm not...I'm Azadeh.

NASIMA. No. You're Nasim. You can do anything now.

AZADEH. Is it worth it?

NASIMA. You can be anyone.

AZADEH. (*Looking down*) Except who I am.

NASIMA. (*Lifting* **AZADEH***'s chin*) Chin up.

Scene Nine

(The Engagement ceremony. **ZEMAN, HODA, AZADEH** *and* **NASIMA** *stand onstage.)*

(Music is heard from offstage. It grows louder and louder.)

*(***YASIR** *enters dressed in his finest, followed by* **LAILA.** **ZEMAN** *shakes* **YASIR***'s hand heartily.* **AZADEH,** *at her father's side, also greets him. The men and women separate, celebrating.)*

*(***NASIMA** *spots* **YASIR** *from where she is standing on the opposite side of the stage. She attempts to exit, prevented only by the hold of* **HODA.** *She bows her head. Propelled by* **HODA,** **NASIMA** *approaches a couch center stage. As she passes, women's voices tease. She forces herself to smile, but cannot raise her head. They make it to the couch and she sits.* **YASIR** *watches her every move. Once she is in place, he approaches her.)*

*(***YASIR** *goes to* **NASIMA.** *Teasing and giggling is heard as he passes.* **YASIR** *sits down next to* **NASIMA** *on the couch and outstretches a hand.* **NASIMA** *hesitatingly puts her clenched right fist into it. He tries to catch a glimpse of her face. She won't look at him. Exaggeratedly, he attempts to open her fist.)*

YASIR. My bride won't relent! Perhaps I have something worthy enough for her.

*(***YASIR** *presents a ring to* **NASIMA.***)*

(She does not budge.)

No! Such a lowly earthly treasure cannot tempt my bride. I must convince her of my devotion.

(This time **YASIR** *attempts to open* **NASIMA***'s hand in earnest.)*

(He finds it harder than he thought.)

(He tries to pass this off as if he were still putting on a show.)

(Eventually, **YASIR** *slides off of the couch and onto his knees.)*

*(***NASIMA** *finally is forced to look into his face.)*

(She allows him to open her fist.)

*(***YASIR** *looks up at* **NASIMA***.)*

Nasim?

(The room freezes.)

*(***HODA** *takes some henna and a white cloth out of the basket. She gestures for* **NASIMA***'s hand. She gives it.* **HODA** *marks her palm. She gestures for* **YASIR***'s hand. He looks around. He meets* **LAILA***'s gaze. He looks back at* **HODA***. He thrusts out his right pinky.* **HODA** *marks it.)*

(The cast begins to shout and dance.)

*(***ZEMAN** *approaches* **YASIR** *singing and clapping.* **YASIR** *bows to him but turns to leave.* **NASIMA** *stands up blocking his path. He avoids her gaze, steps around her, and exits.)*

*(***ZEMAN** *watches* **YASIR** *go.* **HODA** *and the other women sit* **NASIMA** *down and start to decorate her hands. She stares blankly ahead.)*

Blackout

ACT II

(NASIMA's house. NASIMA, bacha posh, is packing a bag. She zips it up and sits down next to it. She takes a crumpled letter out of her pocket. There is a knock on the door. Quickly, NASIMA shoves the letter back into her pocket.)

AZADEH. Nasima! Mama needs you.

(pause)

Are you in there?

(tries the doorknob)

Unlock the door.

(pause)

Come on. You can't hide forever.

(Finally, NASIMA goes over to unlock the door. AZADEH stands in the doorway, bacha posh. She sees the bag.)

(calling for help) Mama!

(NASIMA clamps her hand over her AZADEH's mouth and pulls her into the room. AZADEH struggles to get free.)

NASIMA. Don't make me hurt you.

AZADEH. (through NASIMA's hand): Help! Mama!

NASIMA. Shh!

AZADEH. Let me go!

NASIMA. Only if you keep your mouth shut.

(NASIMA uncovers AZADEH's mouth.)

AZADEH. You can't do this. You'll be beaten!

NASIMA. I'm not going to get caught.

AZADEH. It's not that easy.

NASIMA. Why not? He can!

AZADEH. What are you talking about?

NASIMA. Yasir's going to university.

AZADEH. So?

NASIMA. Without me.

AZADEH. But...that could be years.

NASIMA. (*holding up her hands, showing* **AZADEH** *her henna*) See this? This is my sentence. Not a man. Not a woman. Not a wife. Can't study, can't work, can't be courted. Promised to him. Forced to wait until he wants me.

AZADEH. Why wouldn't he want you?

NASIMA. I'm not waiting.

(**NASIMA** *goes back to packing.*)

AZADEH. But Mama...Baba...

NASIMA. I'm a liability! I was supposed to bring in money not take it away. They can't afford me.

AZADEH. You can't measure everything in afghanis.

NASIMA. Grow up!

AZADEH. No.

NASIMA. You can be married.

AZADEH. Who's going to marry the sister of a runaway? You'd do this to me. To Rasa? Mina?

NASIMA. I don't have a choice.

AZADEH. You're just too selfish to –

NASIMA. Don't.

AZADEH. Do whatever you want just don't take away my chance at happiness!

NASIMA. Happiness? There is so much more.

AZADEH. All I want is right here.

NASIMA. Azadeh...

AZADEH. If you loved us...

NASIMA. This isn't about you.

AZADEH. No. It never is. It's all about what you want, what you need. We're all sick and tired of it.

NASIMA. This solves everyone's problems.

> *(AZADEH steals NASIMA's bag and sits on it.)*

Move.

AZADEH. No.

NASIMA. I won't ask again.

AZADEH. Don't you dare touch me.

NASIMA. Then get out of my way.

AZADEH. You can't make it on your own.

NASIMA. Why not?

AZADEH. You're a woman.

NASIMA. No one's going to find me.

AZADEH. But, it's who you are. You can't deny that.

NASIMA. No. It's not.

AZADEH. What?

NASIMA. This life isn't who I am. It never was.

AZADEH. It is you. It's always been you.

NASIMA. I tried. I really did.

AZADEH. Don't let Yasir...

> *(NASIMA grabs for the backpack.)*

Don't deny everything you are because of some stupid boy.

NASIMA. He isn't –

AZADEH. He ruined us.

NASIMA. He's my friend.

AZADEH. A friend wouldn't do this to you!

NASIMA. I betrayed him.

AZADEH. How?

NASIMA. Isn't it obvious?

AZADEH. If he had any brains he'd of used them, instead of just running off and –

NASIMA. Shut up.

> *(NASIMA takes the backpack. AZADEH blocks the door.)*

AZADEH. How can you stand up for him?

NASIMA. It's none of your business.

AZADEH. He ruined you!

NASIMA. They ruined me!

AZADEH. He knows what he's doing to us.

NASIMA. I don't blame him.

AZADEH. It's his fault.

NASIMA. What choice did he have?

AZADEH. We choose our actions. Allah creates the consequences.

NASIMA. I can't stay.

AZADEH. You'll lose him forever.

NASIMA. I already have.

AZADEH. A bacha posh, educated, beautiful…

NASIMA. Don't kid yourself.

(**NASIMA** *picks up scarves, tying them together.*)

AZADEH. I'm not.

NASIMA. I can't be locked up. I won't be.

AZADEH. If he'd stayed, paid the bride price…would you have married him?

(**NASIMA** *approaches* **AZADEH** *with the scarves.*)

What are you doing?

NASIMA. (*Offering them to* **AZADEH**) I need a head start.

(**AZADEH** *stares at them. She looks up into* **NASIMA**'s *face.*)

(*Slowly, she sits down in the chair.*)

(**NASIMA** *quickly and ties* **AZADEH** *up.*)

Tell Mama, Baba, and the girls goodbye for me.

(**NASIMA** *places a nicely folded letter near* **AZADEH**.)

It's better this way.

(**NASIMA** *kisses* **AZADEH**'s *head. She exits.* **AZADEH** *waits.*)

HODA. (*offstage*) Azadeh?

AZADEH. Baba…

HODA. Nasima? Girls?

> (**HODA** *enters. She rushes over to* **AZADEH** *and unties her.*)

AZADEH. (*calling*) Baba…Baba!

HODA. What's going…? Where's your sister?

> (**HODA** *picks up the letter.* **ZEMAN** *rushes in.*)

ZEMAN. What is it?

AZADEH. I tried to stop her, but…

HODA. Nasima's gone.

> (**ZEMAN** *grabs the letter from* **HODA** *and reads.*)

Should I call…?

ZEMAN. No. No one can find out about this.

> (*to* **AZADEH**)

How long ago did she leave?

AZADEH. Just a few minutes.

> (**ZEMAN** *rifles through the dresser and pulls out a burqa.*)

ZEMAN. (*to* **HODA**) Don't do anything strange. If anyone comes over…Nothing's wrong.

HODA. But what if…

ZEMAN. Don't tell Mina or Rasa. Just in case. Azadeh.

> (**ZEMAN** *motions for* **AZADEH** *to follow him. They turn to leave.*)

> (**HODA** *goes to the window and watches them leave.*)

> (*Finally she falls to her knees in prayer.*)

Scene Two

(YASIR's house. LAILA runs into YASIR.)

YASIR. You knew! Why didn't you tell me?

LAILA. Baba forbid me.

YASIR. Does everyone think I'm stupid? Didn't you think I would recognize him?

LAILA. Her. She's a woman.

YASIR. We all thought he was...

LAILA. Bacha posh. That's the point.

YASIR. He's a girl! How could she do that?

LAILA. Well, she put on some pants. Then she...

YASIR. I'm serious.

LAILA. You know the tradition...it's a blessing to marry one.

YASIR. She lied to me.

LAILA. She told you she was a boy?

YASIR. How did father find her?

(LAILA busies herself with something.)

YASIR. It was you. Wasn't it? How dare you!

LAILA. Father was looking. He asked the family first...I wanted to –

YASIR. And you didn't think I should know?

LAILA. I couldn't!

YASIR. Why?

LAILA. You know why.

YASIR. What was supposed to happen? Were you going to have her wear a burqa until the wedding night?

LAILA. You caught me! It was all a great, horrible plan to trap you into a horrific fate.

YASIR. You thought I'd jump at the chance to marry my best friend?

LAILA. Yes.

YASIR. Why?

LAILA. Why not?

YASIR. Would you would want to marry your best friend?

LAILA. Yes.

YASIR. If he was also a she? I mean if you knew him as a her, but then discovered that she was a he?

LAILA. What?

YASIR. You know what I mean.

LAILA. That would never happen.

YASIR. But if…

LAILA. What could be better?

YASIR. You should have warned me!

LAILA. Would it have made a difference?

YASIR. Yes.

LAILA. Baba already pledged his honor.

YASIR. I'm going to university without her.

LAILA. What?

YASIR. It's settled.

LAILA. How could you do that?

YASIR. I can't marry her!

LAILA. You're a disgrace to our family!

YASIR. You have no right to –

LAILA. Don't throw this away!

YASIR. You think you can say whatever you want. Well you can't. You're a girl.

LAILA. What are you so afraid of?

YASIR. How dare you…

LAILA. You've been offered a great blessing. You know her.

YASIR. Get out.

(**LAILA** *stands her ground.*)

YASIR. I'm your brother and you'll do as I say!

LAILA. You're acting like a child.

YASIR. Every day he let me believe he was something he wasn't.

LAILA. She saved her family!

YASIR. I confided in him! In Nasim!

LAILA. Nasima.

YASIR. A woman.

LAILA. Who should be your wife.

YASIR. She compromised the fundamental part of her being!

(**LAILA** *drops her gaze to the floor but doesn't move.*)

LAILA. Do you know what's going to happen to her?

YASIR. I don't care.

LAILA. Really?

YASIR. What choice did I have?

LAILA. She has nothing now! Are you happy?

YASIR. I can't marry him.

LAILA. Her.

YASIR. Shut up.

LAILA. You're a coward.

(**YASIR** *grabs* **LAILA**, *pulling her off the ground.*)

Be logical for once. Have you seen the way she looks at you?

(**YASIR** *lets her go.*)

YASIR. What?

LAILA. She likes you.

YASIR. No…He can't! We were –

LAILA. Tutoring. Never giving up. She played football even though she hated it…

YASIR. He doesn't hate it.

LAILA. Fine. Even though she wasn't any good at it.

YASIR. Because he was my friend.

LAILA. Because she loves you.

YASIR. No! He can't…She can't…

LAILA. Why not?

YASIR. This isn't how it is supposed to work. I can't look at her without seeing him!

LAILA. It could be worse.

YASIR. Yeah right.

LAILA. Would you rather marry a stranger?

YASIR. Haven't you been listening?

LAILA. Well. Now you'll get your chance.

YASIR. I want to marry a woman.

LAILA. She is a woman.

YASIR. Not to me.

LAILA. Open your eyes.

YASIR. This…it isn't fair! She's had time to adjust.

LAILA. So?

YASIR. She always knew I was a guy. She didn't have to just flip a switch and…

LAILA. Really?

YASIR. Not like…

LAILA. She gave up everything for you. Only last week she was working, tutoring, dreaming of university…

YASIR. You stabbed me in the back.

LAILA. You promised yourself to her.

YASIR. Only to protect our honor!

LAILA. Nice job.

YASIR. Engagements are supposed to be special. Something to tell the grandchildren.

LAILA. This is quite a story.

YASIR. Not the one I wanted.

LAILA. Baba chose her for you.

YASIR. No…You did.

LAILA. They knew who she was to you.

YASIR. You convinced them to take your frustrated love life out on me!

LAILA. This is not about me!

YASIR. You're of age. Why aren't you married? Baba indulged you too long. If I was in charge…

LAILA. Well you're not.

YASIR. One day you're going to have a man to put you in your place. And you won't be able to say anything otherwise.

(She tries to leave. **YASIR** *tries to stop her.)*

YASIR. Laila…

LAILA. So I suppose that's what you wanted? A woman, a doll to wait on you hand a foot? A person to exercise dominion over? Is that marriage? That your idea of love?

YASIR. No, I meant…

LAILA. What is it then? What do you want?

YASIR. Not this.

LAILA. Answer the question.

YASIR. Time…I need more time.

LAILA. There isn't any. You have to act now. What do you want in a wife?

YASIR. I don't know! There. Are you happy?

LAILA. I want love. I want freedom. I want equality. Someone to talk to, to share with. Someone who understands me. A true friend.

YASIR. What about honesty?

LAILA. You want honesty? Stop lying to yourself and open your eyes to what is right in front of you. You have a chance at something that most of us will never have.

YASIR. How do you know that?

LAILA. I know her.

*(***AZADEH*** barges in, dressed in bacha posh.)*

(However, she still moves/motions/reacts like a woman.)

LAILA. What happened?

AZADEH. My father needs to see you.

YASIR. I'm not going to marry Nasim.

LAILA. Nasima.

AZADEH. He's waiting outside. Please.

LAILA. What's wrong?

AZADEH. (*to* **LAILA**) She's gone.

LAILA. (*to* **YASIR**) They'll flog her. In front of everyone.

YASIR. Why come to me?

AZADEH. You made a promise to our family.

YASIR. Which you broke.

LAILA. Yasir.

> (*pause*)

You're the only one who'd know where to find her.

AZADEH. Please.

> (*pause*)

YASIR. Where's your father?

AZADEH. I'll get him.

> (**AZADEH** *exits.* **LAILA** *hugs* **YASIR.**)

YASIR. (*pulling* **LAILA** *off*) When he comes in, take her to your room.

> (**ZEMAN** *enters, handing* **YASIR** **NASIMA**'s *note immediately.* **YASIR** *reads.*)

ZEMAN. She's not downtown or at the store. All of the usual places…

YASIR. Why come to me?

ZEMAN. You're her friend!

YASIR. Nothing more.

ZEMAN. My daughter's out there right now risking her life –

YASIR. Because of me?

ZEMAN. I don't want to fight. I just want my daughter back.

YASIR. You chose the wrong man.

ZEMAN. No I didn't. You care for her.

YASIR. You made her break the law!

ZEMAN. Don't change the subject!

YASIR. I'm not!

ZEMAN. Can you deny the person bacha posh made her?

YASIR. Someone who runs away?

ZEMAN. No. Someone who knows what she wants.

YASIR. Is that a good thing in a woman?

ZEMAN. You tell me.

(*pause*)

YASIR. You should have picked someone else.

ZEMAN. She loves you.

YASIR. She told you that?

ZEMAN. No, but…

YASIR. How do you know?

ZEMAN. She's my daughter.

YASIR. That doesn't mean you can tell!

ZEMAN. I want the best for her.

YASIR. Me?

ZEMAN. I'm not asking you to reconsider. Just bring her back.

(**ZEMAN** *offers* **YASIR** *the burqa. He takes it.*)

YASIR. This doesn't mean I'll marry her. I'm only doing this for him. Nasim.

(**YASIR** *exits.* **ZEMAN** *watches.*)

Scene Three

(NASIMA's house. HODA straightens up ZEMAN's study. ZEMAN enters.)

HODA. Did you – ?   **ZEMAN.** No word?

HODA. Where did you look?

ZEMAN. The store, the school, through the markets...I'll check the depot next.

HODA. Where do you think she'll go?

ZEMAN. Where no one will question her choices.

HODA. The West? She can't!

ZEMAN. Pray she doesn't.

HODA. What do you think I've been doing?

(ZEMAN goes over to HODA.)

ZEMAN. She'll come home.

HODA. If this gets out...

ZEMAN. It won't come to that.

HODA. If she's not back before dark, there's nothing we can do. What about her sisters?

ZEMAN. It's in Allah's hands.

(pause)

I went to Yasir.

HODA. What? He rejected her! He ruined us!

ZEMAN. We can trust him, if he's the man I think he is.

HODA. Zeman!

ZEMAN. Are you doubting our choice?

HODA. It's over. There's no wedding. And she's chosen flogging over her family!

ZEMAN. No one's going to lay a hand on our daughter.

HODA. How can we stop it?

ZEMAN. Trust Allah.

HODA. I wish I had your faith.

ZEMAN. You do. More.

(**HODA** *looks away.*)

ZEMAN. We were young once.

HODA. We understood our responsibility. We didn't act on rash whims.

ZEMAN. No?

HODA. Of course not! Did you?

ZEMAN. There were moments when I...

HODA. Really?

(**ZEMAN** *leans in closer to* **HODA** *as if to kiss her.*)

ZEMAN. But when I saw you, all those wild thoughts fled my mind.

(**HODA** *jumps up to avoid him.*)

HODA. Our daughter's out there and you want to...

ZEMAN. Do you wish you knew me before?

HODA. We don't have time to talk about this.

ZEMAN. Answer me.

HODA. I trusted my parents.

ZEMAN. Then why didn't you talk to me for the first two months?

HODA. It wasn't that long...

ZEMAN. What changed your mind?

HODA. (*Pulling* **ZEMAN** *up*) Go find her.

ZEMAN. Tell me.

(**ZEMAN** *sits determinedly. He pulls her down. They sit close to each other.*)

HODA. You weren't what I expected.

ZEMAN. Oh?

HODA. Patient. Kind.

ZEMAN. You were scared of me?

HODA. I was a child.

ZEMAN. So is she.

HODA. I didn't run away.

ZEMAN. You wanted to.

HODA. How did you – ?

ZEMAN. I wanted to.

HODA. You did?

ZEMAN. Allah has blessed us beyond anything I could have dreamed. He won't turn his back on us now. Sometimes I thank him I wasn't blessed with a son.

HODA. Hold your tongue!

ZEMAN. It's changed my vision. Every man should be so cursed.

HODA. Boys would have been easier.

ZEMAN. Perhaps…

HODA. But daughters…

ZEMAN. When I first saw their faces…Each beautiful girl… It made me fall in love with you all over again. Allah had granted us one of his angels so I promised him… I'd do anything, give anything in the world for them. And I can give them this. I can give them a caring man to share their life.

HODA. Yasir?

ZEMAN. He'll bring her back.

HODA. But will he marry her?

ZEMAN. Yes.

HODA. How can you…?

ZEMAN. Hoda.

HODA. Trust Allah…right. But that girl…Such a headstrong, stubborn…

ZEMAN. Intelligent.

HODA. Proud, outspoken…

ZEMAN. Like her mother.

HODA. Like her father.

ZEMAN. Send them to me, when he brings her back.

(He exits.)

HODA. Our daughters should be so lucky.

Scene Four

(Under a Bridge on the outskirts of the city. NASIMA *enters in bacha posh. She sighs and sits on the ground. She pulls out a map from her sack. She hears a noise behind her. Before she can escape* YASIR *grabs her from behind.* NASIMA *struggles.)*

YASIR. *(disguising his voice, as if calling to others)* I got her! Over here, under the bridge!

NASIMA. Let go!

YASIR. You know the law.

*(*NASIMA *jabs* YASIR *with an elbow. He collapses to the ground and groans.)*

NASIMA. *(turning around to look at him)* Yasir? Where are the others?

*(*YASIR *grabs her foot. They struggle.)*

YASIR. You didn't have to…

NASIMA. You deserved it.

YASIR. For trying to save your life?

NASIMA. For abandoning me.

YASIR. Thought you'd return the favor?

NASIMA. I didn't have a choice.

YASIR. Yeah? What's your excuse now?

NASIMA. None of your business.

*(*NASIMA *picks up her bag.)*

YASIR. Where do you think you're going?

*(*NASIMA *glances at the map.* YASIR *grabs it before she can get it.)*

YASIR. What's your plan?

NASIMA. Give it back!

YASIR. Mountains or desert?

NASIMA. What?

YASIR. Which pass? Mountains or desert?

NASIMA. Does it matter?

YASIR. You want to live?

(using the map to show her)

Refugees use this one. Insurgents camp out over here.

NASIMA. How do you know?

YASIR. One you have the chance of being discovered and shipped back here. The other you'd be raped and killed. Your choice.

NASIMA. You're making this up.

YASIR. How do you think we ship our products?

NASIMA. What about this one?

YASIR. Held by military.

NASIMA. What about the desert?

(YASIR snatches her bag and begins looking through it.)

NASIMA. What are you doing?

YASIR. Looking for a camel or a land rover.

(pulls out a canteen)

Oh, good. This'll last a day or two.

NASIMA. I can find water.

YASIR. Right. Show me.

NASIMA. *(pointing)* There and there.

YASIR. Who controls them?

NASIMA. I don't...

YASIR. Maybe you should try your luck in the mountains.

(NASIMA grabs her bag back and starts repacking.)

NASIMA. Who asked you anyway?

YASIR. You're headed west? Well? Smart.

NASIMA. Women aren't chattel there.

YASIR. No. They're objects of...

NASIMA. They're free.

YASIR. That's what you want?

NASIMA. They can make their own decisions!

YASIR. To turn their back on Allah.

NASIMA. That's not what I'm...

YASIR. Then what are you doing? You were the top of our class.

NASIMA. And that prepared me for what? Having sons?

YASIR. What's wrong with that?

NASIMA. What's wrong with daughters?

YASIR. I didn't mean –

NASIMA. You're just like the rest of them.

YASIR. Hold on a minute!

NASIMA. Why should men get everything while women – ?

YASIR. That's not how it is!

NASIMA. How would you know?

YASIR. I have sisters.

NASIMA. That's different. I've seen both sides.

YASIR. But, I –

NASIMA. You don't know what you're talking about.

YASIR. If you'd just explain it.

NASIMA. I can't!

YASIR. You lied to me.

NASIMA. Bacha posh is a lie!

YASIR. You should have told me.

NASIMA. I couldn't.

YASIR. Why?

NASIMA. I didn't...I was scared.

YASIR. Of what?

NASIMA. This.

YASIR. What are you talking about?

NASIMA. You hate me...I didn't want to...

YASIR. What?

NASIMA. Forget it.

YASIR. Come on...

NASIMA. (*pulling away*) It doesn't matter anymore, okay?

YASIR. What was I supposed to do? Jump for joy?

NASIMA. Go away.

YASIR. No.

NASIMA. Please.

YASIR. How much money do you have?

NASIMA. Some.

YASIR. How much?

> (**NASIMA** *pulls out her money and gives it to* **YASIR**.)

You couldn't bribe a schoolboy with this.

> (**NASIMA** *tries to snatch it back.*)

> (**YASIR** *pulls away.*)

NASIMA. Let me go.

YASIR. Why?

NASIMA. What's back there for me?

YASIR. Your life.

NASIMA. What life? Without you I can't…

YASIR. And what about me?

NASIMA. At least you won't be trapped in a house. You can go to university. Take another wife.

YASIR. I would never…

NASIMA. (*leaving*) I won't be a slave to you…to men.

YASIR. (*holding out her money*) Hey!

> (**NASIMA** *comes back and grabs it from him.*)

I never treated you like that.

NASIMA. Because you thought I was –

YASIR. And Laila?

NASIMA. What about her?

YASIR. I don't treat her like that.

NASIMA. What about when she stands up to you?

YASIR. That's different.

NASIMA. How?

YASIR. Sometimes she just…She knows how to push me and she can't do that.

NASIMA. Why not?

YASIR. She has to respect me.

NASIMA. Why do you get the final say? Because Allah made you a boy.

YASIR. I didn't make the rules.

NASIMA. You follow them.

YASIR. I'm not like other men.

NASIMA. I used to believe that.

(NASIMA *starts to leave.* YASIR *grabs her and forces her to face him.*)

YASIR. Don't think for a second I wouldn't turn you in.

NASIMA. You wouldn't dare.

(YASIR *pushes her away.*)

YASIR. Know any other men who would risk his reputation for a headstrong bacha posh?

NASIMA. You think I wanted this? What does a five-year-old know about anything?

YASIR. Five?

NASIMA. Yeah. One of Laila's crazy friends.

NASIMA	YASIR
Mama told me I could go to school and run and play, do things that none of my sisters got to.	The girl with pencils for legs? The one who caused all sorts of trouble…

NASIMA. Why question?

YASIR. But you had to…when we were…when you…

NASIMA. I didn't want it to end. If I wished, somehow I thought…

YASIR. Yeah.

NASIMA. But they took it all away.

YASIR. Because it wasn't real.

NASIMA. It was the only way I could do any of this!

YASIR. But you can't deny who Allah made you.

NASIMA. What's the real difference between a girl and a boy?

YASIR. Besides the obvious?

NASIMA. Yes.

YASIR. I don't know.

NASIMA. We still yearn for happiness just like...

YASIR. And your instincts?

NASIMA. What?

YASIR. You know...Female instincts?

NASIMA. Like animals?

YASIR. No...like nurturing, motherhood...stuff like that.

NASIMA. And I suppose male instincts are for math and science?

YASIR. Well...

NASIMA. What happened to you then?

YASIR. I didn't say – !

NASIMA. You implied it.

YASIR. How?

NASIMA. Why should gender assign our talents? Do you know how many women don't even try to learn because they believe they can't? I could have gone to university!

YASIR. But –

NASIMA. And don't you want to be a father?

YASIR. Yeah. Sometime.

NASIMA. When did you decide that?

YASIR. I don't know. I guess I always kind of...

NASIMA. But you're a man, men don't want to –

YASIR. All right. I get it.

NASIMA. Baba loves me just as much as Mama.

YASIR. It's not the same.

NASIMA. Yeah. For us it's a requirement. Why would Allah rob me of the freedom to be happy?

YASIR. It isn't Allah.

(pause)

Come back with me.

NASIMA. Why?

YASIR. It'll die down.

NASIMA. That's the real lie.

(NASIMA gathers her things to go.)

YASIR. You didn't want to get married. Did you?

NASIMA. Guess you'll never know.

(NASIMA almost exits.)

YASIR. Nasima!

(She stops abruptly and turns around, looking directly at him. He doesn't move.)

YASIR. What do I tell your family?

NASIMA. That you couldn't find me.

YASIR. I can't lie to them!

NASIMA. Then close your eyes and count to ten.

YASIR. All right. Answer one question...then I'll let you go.

NASIMA. Fine.

YASIR. You have to be completely honest.

NASIMA. Don't insult me.

YASIR. Promise?

NASIMA. Yasir...

YASIR. Do you promise?

NASIMA. Yes. I promise.

YASIR. Your father said something to me...

NASIMA. He says a lot of things.

YASIR. ...when he asked me to find you. Is it true?

NASIMA. Was I there?

YASIR. He said that you...you know...that you had feelings...

NASIMA. For you?

(**YASIR** *nods.*)

What kind of...?

YASIR. Do you?

NASIMA. How? As a friend? A brother? I mean you could be a little more specific.

YASIR. (*cutting her off*) Do you love me Nasima?

NASIMA. Love? What do parents know?

YASIR. Why would he say that?

NASIMA. I don't...

YASIR. You promised.

NASIMA. Do you?

YASIR. I asked you first.

NASIMA. If I tell you...will you promise to tell me?

YASIR. That wasn't part of the deal.

NASIMA. I have a right to know.

YASIR. (*pause*) All right.

NASIMA. Promise?

YASIR. Yes!

NASIMA. Could you love me...the way I need to be loved?

YASIR. (*pause*) Come back.

NASIMA. Answer the question.

YASIR. You first.

NASIMA. No. You.

YASIR. I could just kill you sometimes!

NASIMA. Well get in line! Yes or no?

YASIR. If it's no?

NASIMA. Then I'll leave.

YASIR. I haven't had enough time to even...

NASIMA. Yes or no?

YASIR. You can't put this on me like...

NASIMA. That wasn't an option.

(She hurriedly gathers her things and heads out.)

*(**YASIR** makes no move to stop her.)*

YASIR. Yes.

*(**NASIMA** stops and turns toward him.)*

NASIMA. What?

YASIR. If you give me…

*(**NASIMA** turns to leave again.)*

Yes!

*(Slowly, **NASIMA** returns.)*

NASIMA. Okay.

YASIR. So…?

NASIMA. What?

YASIR. Your turn.

NASIMA. Isn't it obvious?

(He offers the burqa. After a moment she takes it.)

(He takes her bag and turns around while she puts on the burqa.)

I can take that now.

(He turns around and looks at her.)

YASIR. I've got it.

*(**NASIMA** reaches for her bag.)*

NASIMA. But, I can…

*(**YASIR** dodges her, keeping the bag close.)*

YASIR. I know, but…

*(**NASIMA** stops.)*

NASIMA. Thank you.

(They exit together.)

Scene Five

(NASIMA's house. ZEMAN sits on the floor. NASIMA enters followed by YASIR. ZEMAN gets up. She approaches ZEMAN and kneels before him in humility. ZEMAN kneels down and embraces her.)

ZEMAN. In the name of Allah, most Gracious, most Compassionate. Thank you.

(HODA enters and drops to her knees.)

(She begins praying in Arabic.)

NASIMA. Forgive me.

ZEMAN. You're back. That's all I care about. Forgive me?

NASIMA. For what?

ZEMAN. Not treating you as an adult.

NASIMA. Of course, Baba.

(YASIR takes a step forward. ZEMAN stands up to look at him. HODA stops praying.)

ZEMAN. What do you want?

YASIR. Your forgiveness.

(ZEMAN doesn't move. HODA looks away.)

And to claim my bride.

ZEMAN. You were going to cast her aside.

YASIR. I changed my mind.

ZEMAN. How can I trust you?

YASIR. She won't let me do otherwise.

(NASIMA elbows YASIR.)

ZEMAN. Her price has gone up.

NASIMA. Baba!

YASIR. Name it.

ZEMAN. 150,000 afghani.

(HODA gasps. YASIR blinks in shock, but continues on.)

YASIR. Done.

(YASIR *offers the money that he has on his person.*)

ZEMAN. That's not enough.

(NASIMA *takes out money that she has hidden and hands the money to* YASIR.)

YASIR. (*handing the money to* ZEMAN) We'll get you the rest.

(ZEMAN *almost smiles.*)

ZEMAN. (*to* YASIR): It seems I will gain another son. Welcome.

YASIR. Thank you, father.

(ZEMAN *helps them up.*)

(HODA *embraces* NASIMA.)

(*She then escorts her away to dress her in a traditional wedding dress.*)

(LAILA *and* AZADEH *enter to help.*)

(*Meanwhile,* ZEMAN *helps* YASIR *dress in traditional wedding garb.*)

ZEMAN. "Whoever marries a woman for her glory, Allah will not increase his, but will bring him humiliation; whoever marries her for her wealth, Allah will not increase his, but place him in poverty; whoever marries her for ancestral claims, Allah will not increase his, but in meanness; whoever marries a woman for nothing but to cast down his eye and join a relationship, Allah will bless him through her and vise versa." This. This is why we chose you.

(ZEMAN *exits.*)

(YASIR *kneels to pray.*)

(NASIMA *enters from behind him.*)

(*Hearing the rustling of her skirts,* YASIR *begins to turn around.*)

NASIMA. Stop!

YASIR. Why? What's going on?

NASIMA. Promise you won't look.

YASIR. Since when do you care about…?

NASIMA. Please.

YASIR. I can't talk to you like this.

NASIMA. Then listen. I want to go to university with you.

YASIR. You will. As my wife.

NASIMA. No. I want to attend university.

YASIR. Fine.

NASIMA. Don't tease me…

YASIR. I need you to. You know…to help me with math.

NASIMA. Right.

YASIR. It's a part of who you are, Nasima. I'd never keep that from you.

NASIMA. After tonight, I'm…I'm yours.

YASIR. I know.

NASIMA. That's a good thing right?

YASIR. Yes.

NASIMA. With all my imperfections?

YASIR. And me in mine?

NASIMA. Equals under Allah?

YASIR. Always.

> (**NASIMA** *touches* **YASIR**'s *shoulder and turns him around to face her.*)

> (**YASIR** *looks at her for the first time. She smiles.*)

> (*Music floods in. A decorated couch on a platform is brought in.* **HODA** *takes* **NASIMA** *by the shoulders and guides her to the couch.* **NASIMA** *sits.*)

> (**ZEMAN**, **LAILA** *and* **AZADEH** *enter. The stage is filled with laughter and excitement.*)

> (*The music shifts.* **YASIR** *looks at* **NASIMA**. *He approaches the platform, steps onto it, and goes over to* **NASIMA**. *She*

offers her hand, which he takes and pulls her up. They turn their backs to the couch.)

(He begins to sit, but once he gets half way down he pops back up.)

(NASIMA is surprised. Then NASIMA does the same. Finally, they both sit down at the exact same time.)

(NASIMA smiles and looks into YASIR's eyes as he puts an arm around her. Their families watch them and cheer.)

Blackout